Bond Book ☑️

This book is part of a special purchase plan
to upgrade the CALS collection. Funds for
the project were approved by Little Rock
voters on 12/11/07. Thanks, Little Rock!

FEB   2014

Winnie Finn, Worm Farmer

Carol Brendler • Pictures by Ard Hoyt

Farrar Straus Giroux

New York

To Ralph and Nikolai, who saved their kitchen scraps
and kept their fingers crossed
—C.B.

To my big sister Brooke, for showing me how to hatch
frog eggs and catch crawdads. You were one heck of a
tomboy once and one terrific big sister always
—A.H.

Text copyright © 2009 by Carol Brendler
Pictures copyright © 2009 by Ard Hoyt
All rights reserved
Distributed in Canada by Douglas & McIntyre Ltd.
Color separations by Embassy Graphics
Printed in February 2009 in China by South China Printing Company Ltd.,
Dongguan City, Guangdong Province
Designed by Jay Colvin
First edition, 2009
1 3 5 7 9 10 8 6 4 2

www.fsgkidsbooks.com

Library of Congress Cataloging-in-Publication Data
Brendler, Carol.
    Winnie Finn, worm farmer / Carol Brendler ; pictures
by Ard Hoyt.— 1st ed.
        p. cm.
    Summary: Winnie Finn raises earthworms, which help
her neighbors win prizes at the county fair. Includes
instructions on making a worm farm.
    Includes bibliographical references.
    ISBN-13: 978-0-374-38440-1
    ISBN-10: 0-374-38440-1
    [1. Earthworms—Fiction.] I. Hoyt, Ard, ill. II. Title.

PZ7.B7512 Wi 2009
[E]—dc22

                                         2008004255

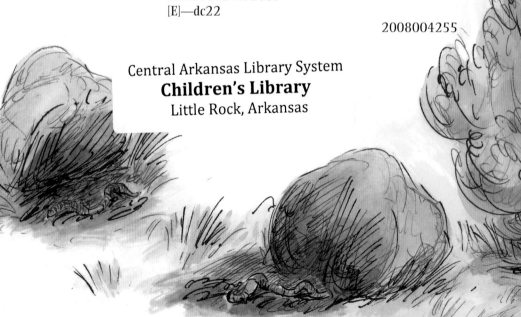

Winnie Finn was earthworm crazy. She turned over stones all around Quincy County in hopes of meeting squirmy worms.

After a rain, Winnie found worms on sidewalks and coaxed them back into their holes.

On cloudy days she took them for rides in her rickety wagon.

And sometimes she even raced them.

Winnie Finn knew that the biggest earthworm ever was ten feet long. She knew that an earthworm has five hearts. And she knew which end was its head and which was its tail because the head always goes first when it moves.

When spring came to Quincy County, Winnie started thinking about the Quincy County Fair. The fair had prizes for things like the best-looking puppies, the best-laying hens, and the best-growing cornstalks.

Winnie Finn wanted to win a prize, too. With the prize money, she could get herself a brand-new wagon. Did they have a prize at the Quincy County Fair for the best worms?

"Worms?" said Mr. Abernathy. "Nonsense! There's no prize for worms. This year, I'm raising corn. With the right fertilizer, my stalks will shoot up high enough to pluck their own raindrops from the clouds! If only I knew what the right fertilizer was. I'd share my prize with anyone who could bring me some."

"Worms!" said Mrs. Yamasaki-O'Sheridan. "Don't be silly. There's no prize for worms. I'm raising Plymouth Rock hens this time. With the right feed, they'll lay so many eggs we'll be eating omelets the size of rubber rafts for breakfast! If only I knew what the right feed was. I'd share my prize with anyone who could find it for me."

"Worms?" said Mr. Peasley. "Are you sure, Winnie? I don't think there is a prize for worms. This summer, I'm raising Afghan pups. If I can make their coats smooth and sleek as slipper satin, they're sure to win a prize. If only I knew how to give them shiny coats. I'd share my prize with anyone who could tell me that."

Winnie Finn knew how to find the right corn fertilizer and the right chicken feed. And she knew how to give puppies shiny coats. It all started with worms.

So she borrowed a seed crate from Mr. Abernathy, who reminded her, "You can't pin a blue ribbon on a worm."

And when she asked Mrs. Yamasaki-O'Sheridan for some chicken manure, *she* said, "There's no worm trophy, young lady."

And when she asked to borrow Mr. Peasley's washtub that he used for bathing his puppies, *he* said, "There's no 'Best in Show' for worms, Winnie Finn."

But Winnie didn't pay them any mind. Soon she'd be sharing their prizes. Soon she'd have a brand-new wagon.

"First, I'll make a worm farm," said Winnie Finn. She filled Mr. Abernathy's crate with soil, strips of newspaper, and leaves. That would be the worms' house.

She mixed in Mrs. Yamasaki-O'Sheridan's chicken manure. That would be the worms' food.

Then she filled Mr. Peasley's washtub with water and poured it over everything. "This will keep the worms moist and help them breathe," said Winnie Finn.

Winnie found all the red wigglers she could. She spread them over their new home and watched them slither into the soil.

For weeks, Winnie Finn watered her worm farm. She fed the worms eggshells, coffee grounds, and carrot peelings. She took them for walks and she sang to them. She even tried to give all of them names, but it was hard to tell them apart—even for Winnie Finn.

Finally, the worm farm was ready. Winnie found Mr. Abernathy watering his corn crop. "I have a present for you, Mr. Abernathy," she said. "Spread this around your corn. You'll have cornstalks tall enough to pluck their own raindrops from the clouds!"

Sure enough, a few weeks later, the corn was taller than Winnie.

"Winnie Finn, you were right! Worm fertilizer was just what this corn needed. How can I thank you?"

"Some corn would be nice, Mr. Abernathy."

Winnie took the corn to Mrs. Yamasaki-O'Sheridan. "I have something for you," she said. "Feed this fresh corn to your hens. You'll have plenty of eggs for omelets the size of rubber rafts for breakfast!"

Sure enough, a couple of weeks later, Mrs. Yamasaki-O'Sheridan's hens were laying so many eggs that she had to scramble to keep up.

"My goodness, Winnie Finn! Fresh corn was just what my darlings needed. How ever can I thank you?"

"With eggs, please, Mrs. Y-O."

Winnie Finn gave the eggs to Mr. Peasley. "Mix these in with your puppies' food," she told him. "They'll have coats as smooth and sleek as slipper satin."

"Thank you, Winnie! You are so clever. I'll mix some up right this minute."

On the day of the Quincy County Fair, everybody came to see who would take first prizes. Winnie kept her fingers crossed for the judging of the tallest cornstalk, the best egg layer, and the prettiest puppy.

And Mr. Abernathy's cornstalks, Mrs. Yamasaki-O'Sheridan's Plymouth Rock hens, and Mr. Peasley's Afghan pups all took first prizes . . .

thanks to Winnie Finn and her worm farm.

With her share of the prize money, Winnie picked out the best new wagon in Quincy County. And on her way home, she couldn't help but notice . . .

Mrs. Alluvial's drooping dahlias . . .

Mr. Yorkington-Smith-Smythe's second-rate Rhode Island Reds . . .

and Mrs. Marcantony's lackluster Lhasa apsos.

Winnie would have to find more worms.

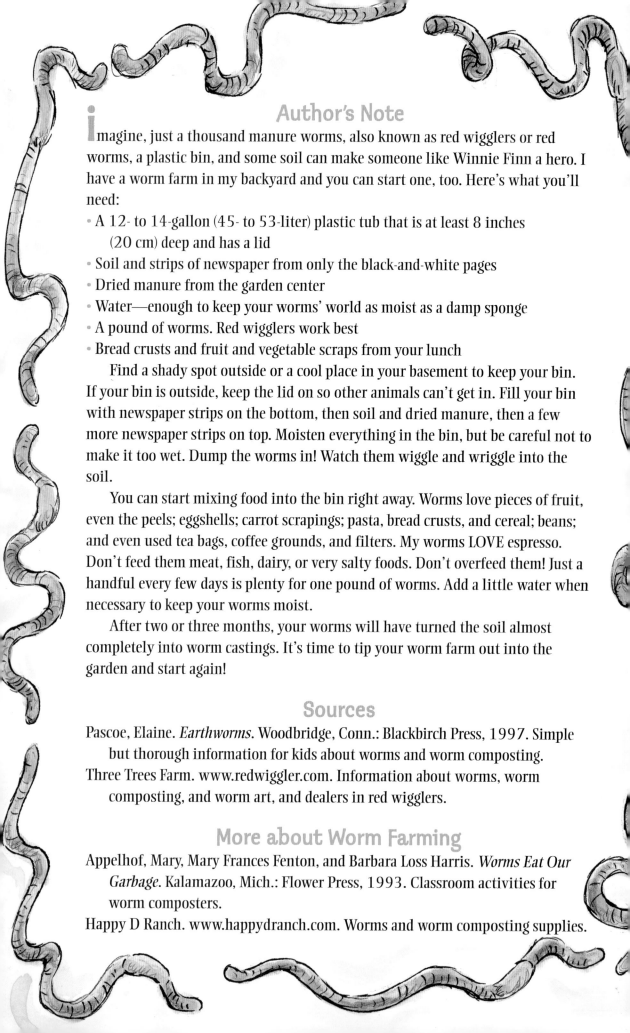

Author's Note

Imagine, just a thousand manure worms, also known as red wigglers or red worms, a plastic bin, and some soil can make someone like Winnie Finn a hero. I have a worm farm in my backyard and you can start one, too. Here's what you'll need:

- A 12- to 14-gallon (45- to 53-liter) plastic tub that is at least 8 inches (20 cm) deep and has a lid
- Soil and strips of newspaper from only the black-and-white pages
- Dried manure from the garden center
- Water—enough to keep your worms' world as moist as a damp sponge
- A pound of worms. Red wigglers work best
- Bread crusts and fruit and vegetable scraps from your lunch

Find a shady spot outside or a cool place in your basement to keep your bin. If your bin is outside, keep the lid on so other animals can't get in. Fill your bin with newspaper strips on the bottom, then soil and dried manure, then a few more newspaper strips on top. Moisten everything in the bin, but be careful not to make it too wet. Dump the worms in! Watch them wiggle and wriggle into the soil.

You can start mixing food into the bin right away. Worms love pieces of fruit, even the peels; eggshells; carrot scrapings; pasta, bread crusts, and cereal; beans; and even used tea bags, coffee grounds, and filters. My worms LOVE espresso. Don't feed them meat, fish, dairy, or very salty foods. Don't overfeed them! Just a handful every few days is plenty for one pound of worms. Add a little water when necessary to keep your worms moist.

After two or three months, your worms will have turned the soil almost completely into worm castings. It's time to tip your worm farm out into the garden and start again!

Sources

Pascoe, Elaine. *Earthworms*. Woodbridge, Conn.: Blackbirch Press, 1997. Simple but thorough information for kids about worms and worm composting.

Three Trees Farm. www.redwiggler.com. Information about worms, worm composting, and worm art, and dealers in red wigglers.

More about Worm Farming

Appelhof, Mary, Mary Frances Fenton, and Barbara Loss Harris. *Worms Eat Our Garbage*. Kalamazoo, Mich.: Flower Press, 1993. Classroom activities for worm composters.

Happy D Ranch. www.happydranch.com. Worms and worm composting supplies.